CRANBERRY EASTER

Wende and Harry Devlin

FOUR WINDS PRESS
New York

Four Winds Press, Macmillan Publishing Company
866 Third Avenue, New York, NY 10022
Collier Macmillan Canada, Inc.
Printed and bound in Japan
First American Edition 10 9 8 7 6 5 4 3 2 1

The text of this book is set in 14 point Baskerville.
The illustrations are rendered in watercolor.

Library of Congress Cataloging-in-Publication Data
Devlin, Wende.
Cranberry Easter/Wende and Harry Devlin. – 1st American ed.
p. cm.
Summary: Events at Easter time convince Seth, owner of
Cranberryport's general store, that he is needed in town and
should change his plans to retire and leave. Includes a
recipe for cranberry cobbler.
ISBN 0-02-729935-X
[1. Easter – Fiction.] I. Devlin, Harry. II. Title.
PZ7.D49875Cpa 1990 [E] – dc19 88-21370 CIP AC

For Alexandra Wende Devlin

"Look! Spring is here." Mr. Whiskers stood at the
door of Seth's General Store with a mass of pussy
willows in his arms.

"I've come to plan your Easter egg hunt, Seth,"
he said. "You dye the eggs this year, and I'll play the
Easter bunny."

Seth frowned. "No! No Easter egg hunt this year. I'm going to sell the store and head south. I'll be gone by Easter time."

"Sell the store!" Mr. Whiskers could not believe his ears. "Suffering codfish, Seth! Who is going to sell me

nightshirts and long underwear? Who am I going to beat at checkers on Saturday nights?"

"It won't be me!" Seth shook his head. "Nobody really needs me. Nobody cares. I'm all alone in this big place. I'm ready to say good-bye to Cranberryport."

This had been a long, lonely winter for Seth. His wife had died in late summer, and he missed the sound of a voice at night. Mr. Whiskers wished he could cheer him, but he couldn't think of a thing to say.

"And I'm tired of all the gray skies," said Seth. He waved good-bye to Mr. Whiskers, banged the door shut, and went off to take a nap in the back of the store.

Mr. Whiskers stopped at Grandmother and Maggie's
house to share his news.

"I'm upset, too," said Grandmother, bustling about
making hot chocolate. "My friends Nan and Grandma
Gates have both decided they can't last another snow-
bound winter alone on their farms. They need rooms
in town, but there are none to be found."

"I have an idea, Grandmother," Maggie cried. "The rooms over Seth's General Store used to be a hotel. Wouldn't they be just right for your friends?"

Mr. Whiskers looked at Maggie in wonder. "You've got it, Maggie!" he boomed. "They are filled with old furniture. We'll get Seth to clear them out."

Grandmother gave Maggie a delighted smile. "I'll start with some calls," she said, and hurried down the hall to the phone.

Overjoyed, Mr. Whiskers hastened back to Seth's General Store.

But Seth turned his back on the whole idea.

"Never!" he grumbled. "I'm much too tired to clean up all those rooms."

Mr. Whiskers wouldn't give up. "Suffering codfish, Seth, these old folks are all alone. Somebody's got to help. They need you!" He paced back and forth.

"Well," said Seth, "it's a jumble upstairs, but maybe we can take a look."

From then on, Mr. Whiskers took charge. After the sale of extra chairs and tables, there was enough money for paint and brushes.

Even the mayor and the sheriff joined in scrubbing,
painting, and polishing. Maggie and her friends
cleaned windows, and Grandmother sewed curtains.

The rooms, bright and clean, were a joyous surprise when Mr. Whiskers, Maggie, and Grandmother showed them to the new residents. Grandma Gates was especially pleased. "I'll never have to go out in a storm for groceries again," she said with great cheer.

Nan looked out the window on the town square. "Oh, Seth! We can watch the Easter egg hunt from here," she said.

Seth threw up his hands. "You win," he told Mr. Whiskers. "I guess I'll have to stay in Cranberryport a little longer. Maggie, tell the children at school the Easter egg hunt is on for sure."

The trees began to bud, and soon there was a magical green mist all over the land. At the General Store, Seth found himself listening now and then for the bustling sounds from overhead. On Easter eve, Grandma Gates helped Seth dye the eggs.

Easter dawned with a brilliant sun in Cranberryport.

Early in the day Seth and Mr. Whiskers began to hide
eggs of every hue—orange, yellow, violet—behind
bushes and trees and under rocks in the village green.

Seth felt a small stir of happiness at being part of this
Easter celebration. "Look at the blue skies today," he
said thoughtfully to Mr. Whiskers.

At noon, a crowd of happy, noisy children began to gather in the center of the village. Mr. Whiskers rounded them up and readied them for the hunt. He called, "One, two, three, GO!"

The Easter egg hunt was on. Children darted among rocks and bushes in search of eggs. They knew that one prize—a large chocolate egg wrapped in gold—awaited the child who found the most.

When nearly all the eggs had been discovered, Seth searched out Mr. Whiskers and whispered a message in his ear. Mr. Whiskers's eyes rolled. He groaned.

"You promised," said Seth as he steered his friend toward the store.

A few moments later a big, fat Easter bunny hopped across the square. The shouting children swarmed all around him.

"What is it?" asked a small boy, pulling on the bunny's tail.

"Suffering codfish, I'm the Easter bunny," Mr. Whiskers shouted. "Can't you see?" Over his head he held a giant basket with chocolate eggs wrapped in gold.

"Today there are prizes for everyone," Seth announced. The children cheered. Even the youngest was given a great golden prize to take home.

"This was the best Easter egg hunt ever!" one of the children shouted to Seth as they waved good-bye.

Seth beamed. "See you next year," he called.

"Next year! Did you hear that?" Mr. Whiskers wheeled around and grinned at Grandmother. "Seth is here to stay."

He started to hop back to dress for Grandmother's
dinner, but then he stopped. Maggie was telling Seth
what they would be having for their Easter feast.

"There'll be roast lamb, new potatoes, mint jelly, and
cranberry cobbler," she said.

"Hooray!" shouted Mr. Whiskers.

"Oh, that's just for us," said Grandmother, winking
at Seth. "For you there is a bunch of carrots back at the
rabbit hutch."

Mr. W······rs began to smile. You couldn't fool him.
There would always be a place at Grandmother's table
for him on holidays—and a place for Seth, too.

He knew friends always take care of one another.
That's the way it is in Cranberryport—on holidays and
the whole year round.

Cranberry Cobbler

(Ask Mother or Father to help)

Filling

3 cups of fresh cranberries
¾ cup of sugar
½ cup of chopped walnuts or pecans

Butter a 10-inch pie plate, spread cranberries over the bottom, and sprinkle with sugar and chopped walnuts or pecans. Stir together right in the pie plate and smooth out.

Crust

2 eggs
¾ cup of sugar
¾ cup of flour
¾ cup of butter, cut in small pieces with a knife

Beat eggs in a bowl until light. Continue to beat, and gradually add first the sugar and then the flour. Finally, cut in the butter.

When crust mixture is thoroughly combined and smooth, spread over filling mixture. Bake at 325° for 45 minutes, or until crust browns.

Serve hot or cold, with or without whipped cream.